Drago

Apple-Picking Day

Adapted by Janie Stevens
Based on an original TV episode written by Steve Westren

SCHOLASTIC INC.
New York Toronto London Auckland
Sydney Mexico City New Delhi Hong Kong

ISBN 978-0-545-20061-5

Published by Scholastic Inc. SCHOLASTIC and associated logos are trademarks and/or registered trademarks of Scholastic Inc.

12 11 10 9 8 7 6 5 4 3 2 1 12 13 14 15 16 17/0

Printed in the U.S.A. 40
First printing, July 2012

One morning, Dragon ate breakfast.

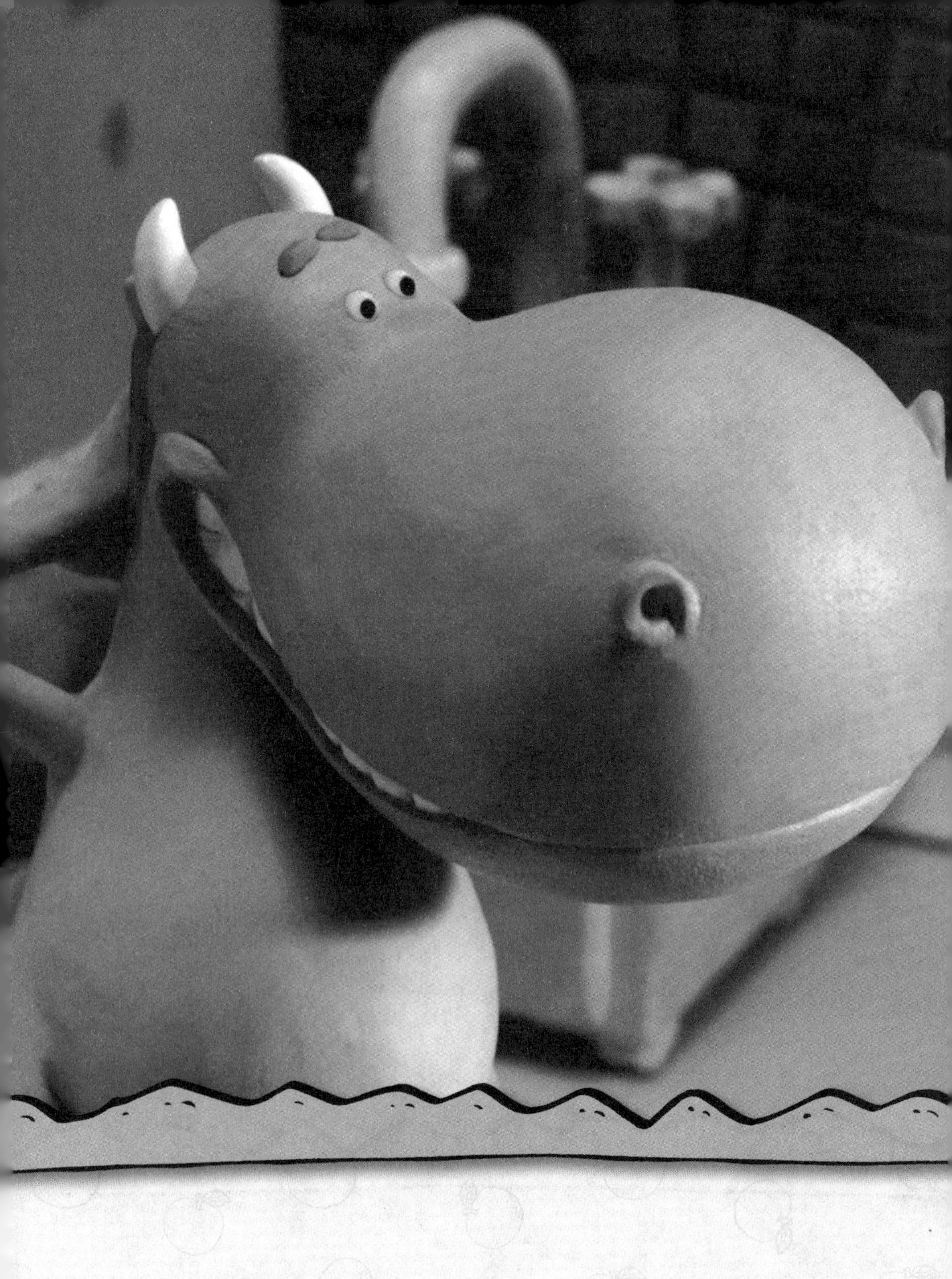

"It is a great day for
apple picking!" said Dragon.

"I am going to pick one apple
for each of my friends," Dragon said.

Dragon walked outside.

He saw four apples hanging from a tree.

Dragon picked one apple.
"Here's one for Alligator," he said.

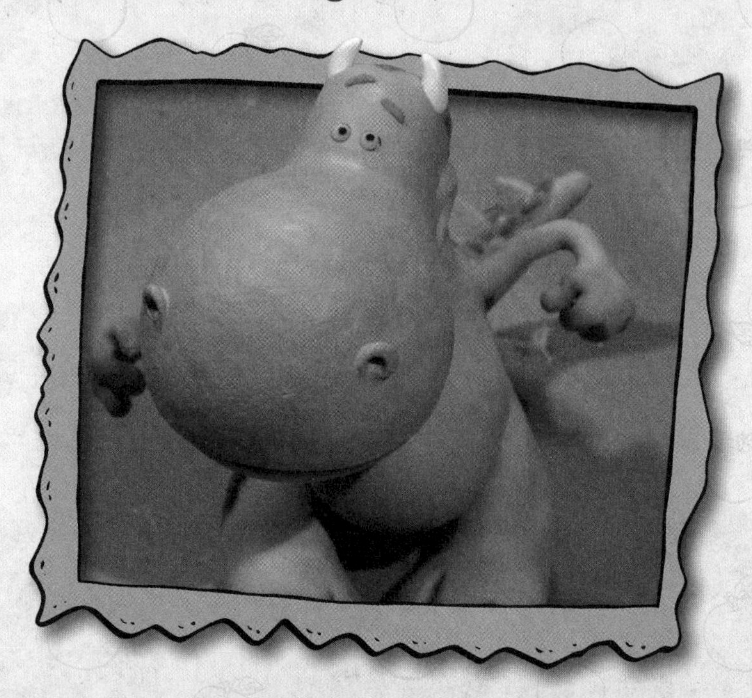

Dragon picked two more apples.
"One for Beaver and
one for Mailmouse!"

But Dragon could not reach
the fourth apple!

"I will blow air on the apple," said Dragon. "Then it will fall."

But the apple
did not fall down.

"I know!" said Dragon.

“I will shake the tree.”

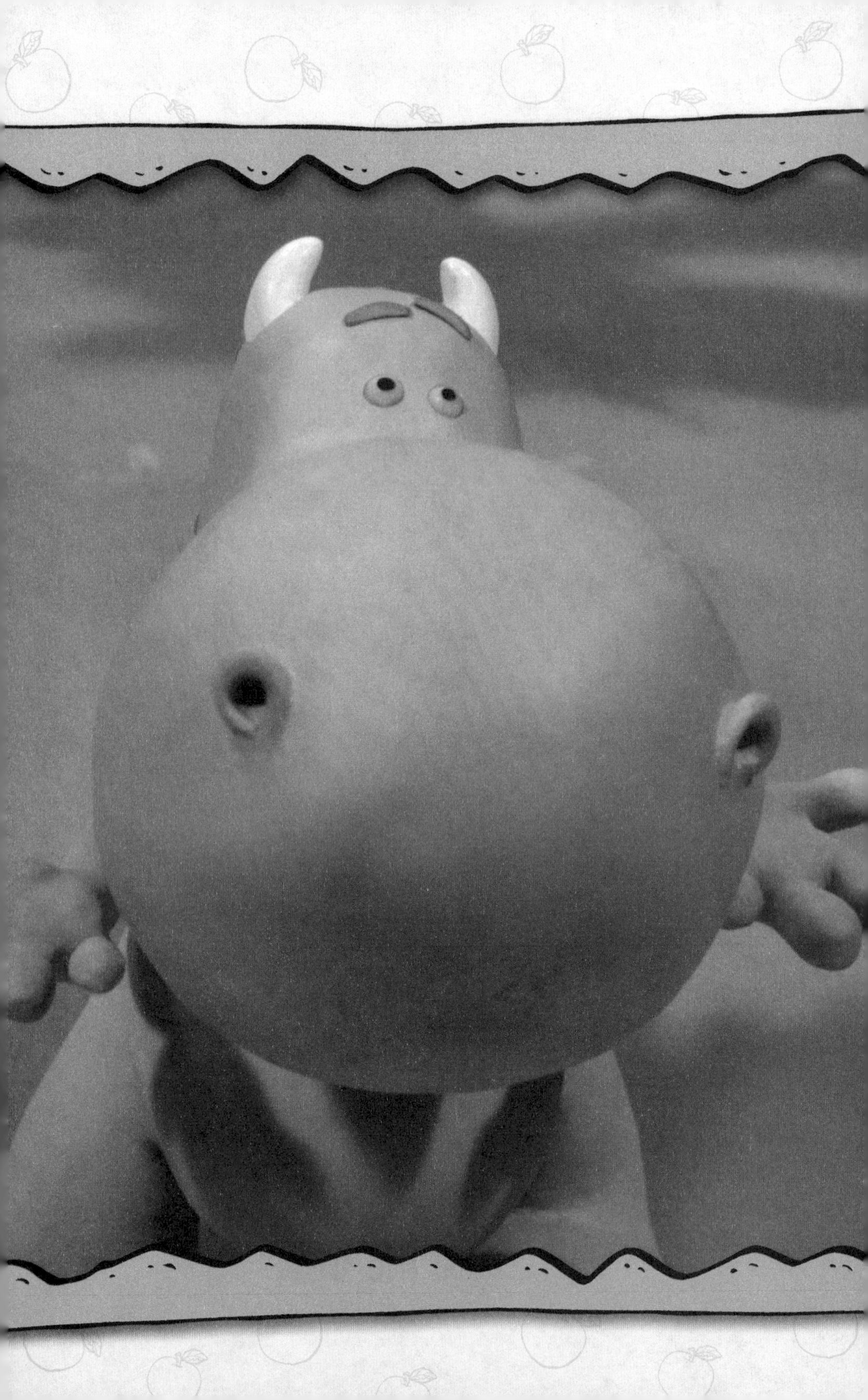

But the apple did not fall down.

"I will wait for the apple
to drop," Dragon said.

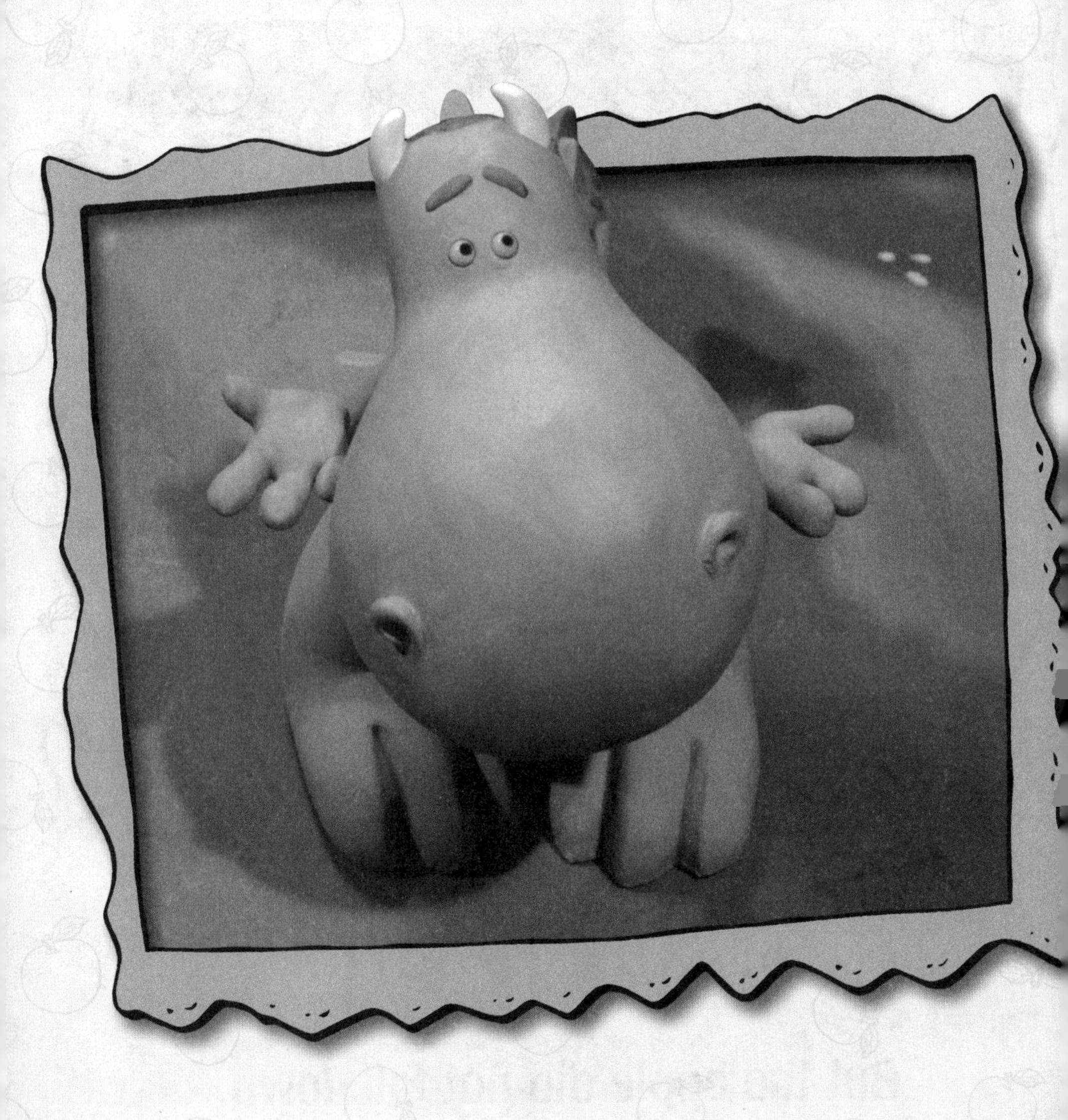

Dragon waited and waited.

But Dragon got tired of waiting.

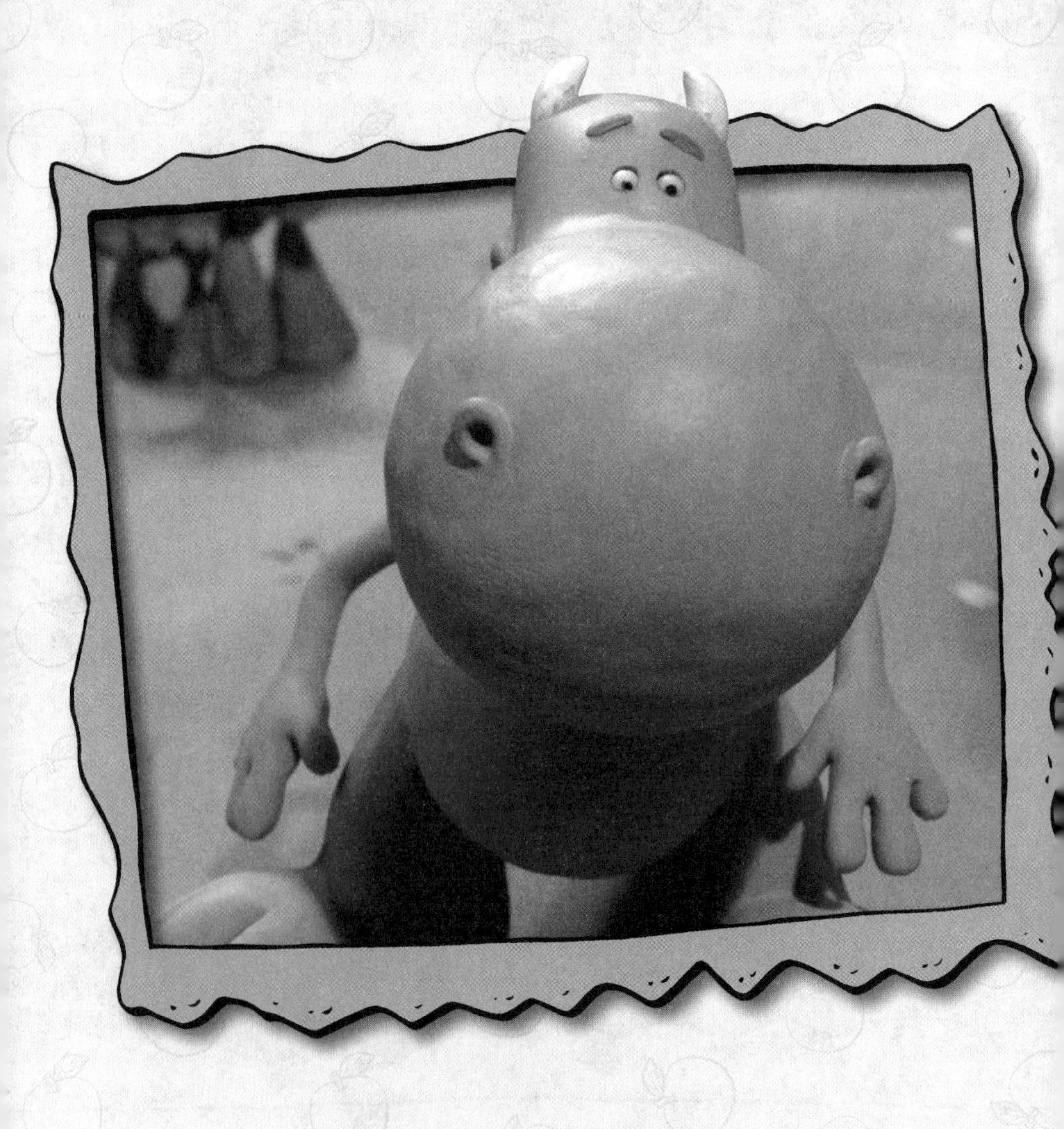

"Maybe the apple
does not want to get hurt,"
said Dragon.

Dragon gave the apple a pillow.

"Here you go, Apple," he said.

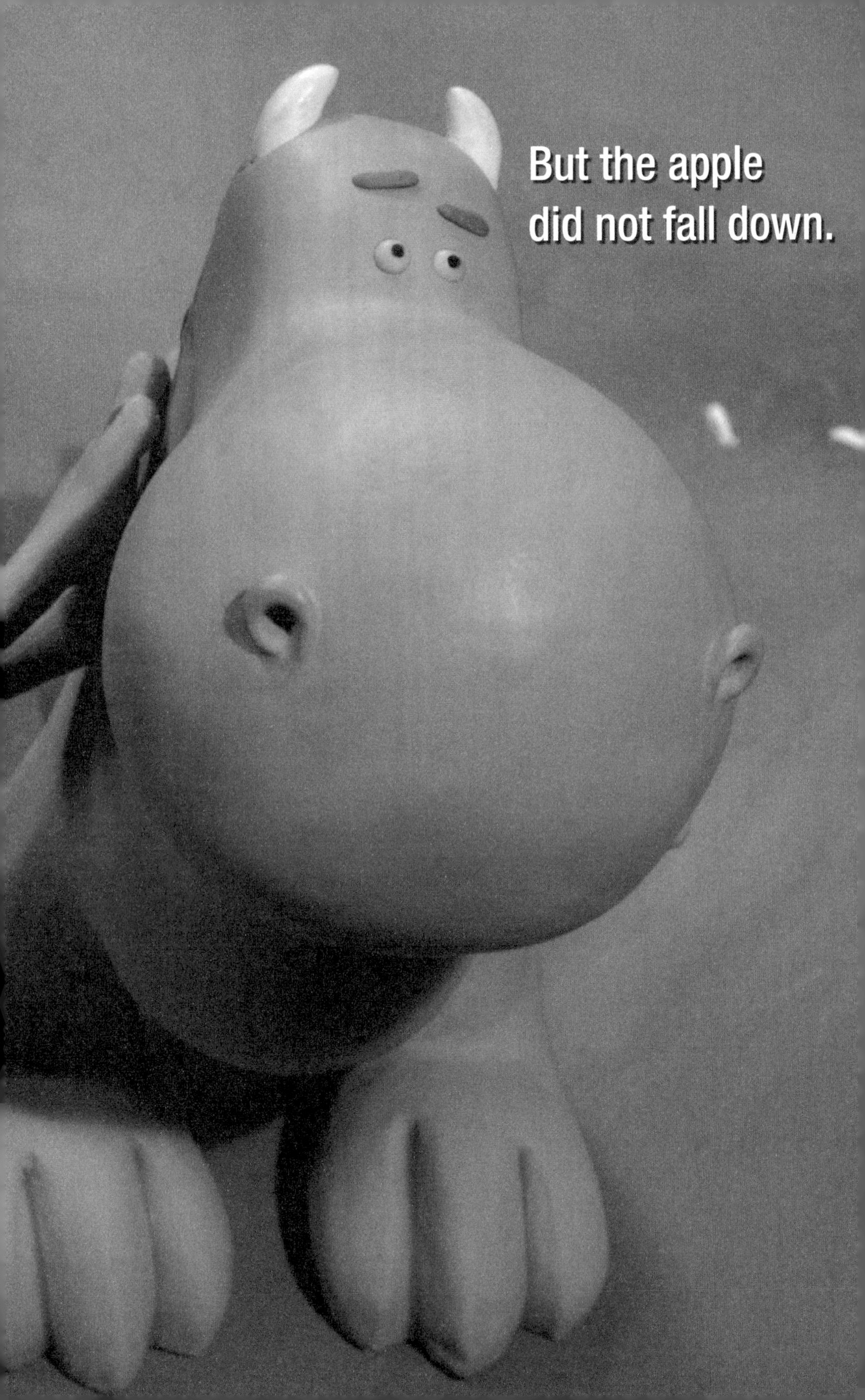
But the apple
did not fall down.

“I have an idea!” Dragon said. “I will scare the apple. Then it will fall down.”

Dragon put on his scary costume.

Then he jumped at the apple.

But the apple did not fall down.

Then Ostrich came to visit.
He saw the apple in the tree.

Ostrich thought the apple was going to fall on Dragon.
Ostrich tried to push Dragon away.

But Dragon bumped into the tree.

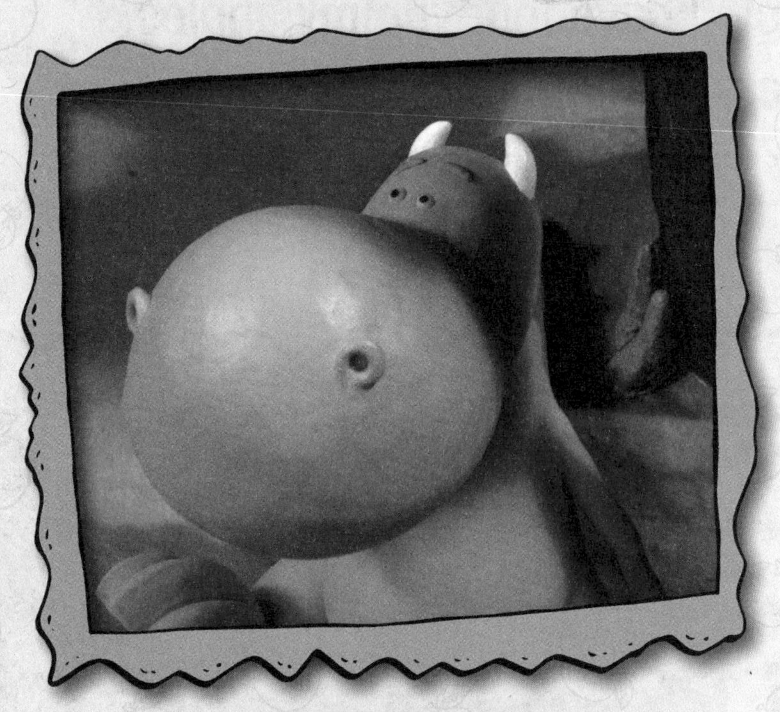

Then the apple fell down!

"Now I have four yummy apples.
There is one for each of
my friends!" Dragon said.